From an episode of the animated TV series *Franklin* produced by Nelvana Limited, Neurones France s.a.r.l. and Neurones Luxembourg S.A., based on the Franklin books by Paulette Bourgeois and Brenda Clark.

TV tie-in adaptation written by Sharon Jennings and illustrated by Mark Koren, Alice Sinkner and Jelena Sisic.

Based on the TV episode *Franklin and Otter's Visit*, written by Ken Ross.

Franklin is a trademark of Kids Can Press Ltd.
The character Franklin was created by Paulette Bourgeois and Brenda Clark.
Text © 2002 Contextx Inc.
Illustrations © 2002 Brenda Clark Illustrator Inc.

Kids Can Press acknowledges the support of the Ontario Arts Council, the Canada Council for the Arts and the Government of Canada, through the BPIDP, for our publishing activity.

Published in Canada by
Kids Can Press Ltd.
29 Birch Avenue
Toronto, ON M4V 1E2

Published in the U.S. by
Kids Can Press Ltd.
2250 Military Road
Tonawanda, NY 14150

www.kidscanpress.com

Edited by Tara Walker and Jennifer Stokes

Printed in Hong Kong, China, by Wing King Tong Company Limited

CM 02 0 9 8 7 6 5 4 3 2

National Library of Canada Cataloguing in Publication Data

Jennings, Sharon
    Franklin and Otter's visit

(A Franklin TV storybook)
The character Franklin was created by Paulette Bourgeois and Brenda Clark.

ISBN 1-55337-021-X

I. Koren, Mark II. Sinkner, Alice III. Sisic, Jelena IV. Bourgeois, Paulette
V. Clark, Brenda VI. Title.

PS8569.E563F71458 2002   jC813'.54   C2001-903737-6
PZ7J429877Fro 2002

Kids Can Press is a Corus™ Entertainment company

Franklin and Otter's Visit

Kids Can Press

FRANKLIN had lots of good friends and a best friend named Bear. He also had a friend named Otter, who had moved away. Franklin and Otter sent each other birthday cards and photographs, but they hadn't seen one another for a long time. Then, one day, a very special letter arrived for Franklin. Otter was coming to visit.

Franklin hurried to Bear's house with his news.

"Guess what?!" he exclaimed. "Otter's coming to stay with her grandma this weekend!"

"Hooray!" said Bear.

"Remember the old days when we used to slip and slide down the riverbank?" Franklin asked.

"Gee, Franklin," replied Bear. "Nobody does *that* anymore."

"Well, I bet Otter will want to," said Franklin.

On his way home, Franklin stopped by the pond. He told Beaver about Otter's visit.

"Remember all the swimming races we used to have?" Franklin asked. "I bet Otter can't wait to race us again."

"Otter is captain of a swim team now," replied Beaver. "She won't want to race us slowpokes."

"Yes, she will," Franklin insisted.

Beaver rolled her eyes.

When he got home, Franklin went to his room.
He searched and searched through his toy box,
under his dresser and in his closet. Then he called
his mother.

"Where are my blocks?" he asked.

"You gave them to Harriet," she answered.
"You said you didn't need them anymore."

"Well, now I want them back," said Franklin.
"Otter and I always played with those blocks."

He marched off to Harriet's bedroom.

Finally, the big day arrived. Otter was coming for lunch.

Franklin sat on the front steps all morning.

"When is she going to get here?" he said over and over. "I can't wait."

And suddenly, there was Otter, walking through the gate.

Franklin and his family gave Otter a big hug and a big welcome. His parents asked her lots of questions about her new home.

Franklin got out the food. "We made happy-face sandwiches just for you," he said.

"I thought those were for Harriet," said Otter.

"They're your favourite," Franklin reminded her.

Otter laughed. "That was *ages* ago."

She took a sandwich from the grown-up plate.

Franklin frowned.

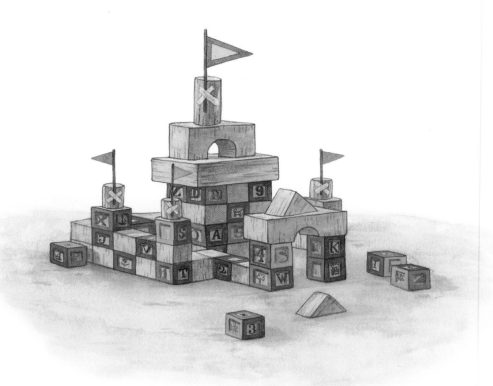

After lunch, Franklin suggested they play with his blocks.

"Remember all the castles we used to build?" he asked.

Otter nodded and followed Franklin to his bedroom. Harriet was already there. She had all the blocks in her lap.

"Mine!" she said.

"I guess blocks are for babies," said Otter.

"I guess," Franklin mumbled.

Franklin and Otter went outside to play.
"Do you still go to the pond?" asked Otter.
"Of course I do," said Franklin. "Let's go!
Everyone will be there."

Franklin was right. They got to the pond, and
the whole gang was excited to see Otter. Beaver
wanted to know how many swimming medals Otter
had won. Franklin suggested they have a race.

"Oh, Franklin," said Beaver. "Otter's too good
a swimmer for us now."

But Franklin was already in the pond.
Otter jumped in beside him.
"Ready. Set. Go!" cried Bear.
Otter was across the pond before Franklin had
swum three strokes.
"Told you so," said Beaver.
Everybody laughed, even Franklin.

Franklin climbed out of the pond.

"Let's play baseball," he suggested.

"I haven't played baseball since I moved," said Otter. "I won't be any good."

Sure enough, Otter struck out on all her turns at bat, and she didn't catch a single ball heading her way.

"I don't want to play anymore," said Otter.

Franklin looked at Otter and sighed.

Just then, Otter's grandma came to get her.

"Will you play with me tomorrow, Franklin?" Otter asked.

"I guess so," replied Franklin.

Otter left, and Franklin walked home alone.

"Hmmphf!" he muttered. "We sure didn't play much today."

Franklin stomped into his house.

"Otter's no fun anymore," he announced. He told his mother about his afternoon.

His mother gave him a hug.

"You've both grown up a bit," she told him. "You've both changed."

"Does that mean we can't be friends anymore?" Franklin asked.

"Maybe," replied his mother. "Or maybe you can find a new way to stay friends."

"Hmmm," said Franklin.

The next morning, Franklin called on Otter bright and early.

"If you still lived in Woodland," Franklin told her, "you'd be a really good baseball player by now."

Then he added, "I'm going to teach you, so every time you visit, you can play on my team."

"Okay," agreed Otter. "And I'm going to teach you to be a faster swimmer. That way, every time I visit, you can race me."

The two friends smiled at each other.

Franklin and Otter spent the day racing in the pond and hitting balls out of the park.

"Today was fun," said Franklin.

"And it was fun yesterday remembering all the things we used to do together," Otter said.

"It was?" asked Franklin.

Otter nodded.

"But I remember something I guess you've forgotten," she said.

Otter grabbed Franklin's hand and pulled him
up to the top of the hill. And together, the two friends
went slipping and sliding down the riverbank and into
the water.

Franklin laughed.

It was just like the old days.